PRAIRIES

PRAIRIES

PETER MURRAY

THE CHILD'S WORLD®, INC.

PHOTO CREDITS

Comstock: 6
Dembinsky Photo Associates/Mike Barlow: 13, 24
Dembinsky Photo Associates/Dominique Braud: 26
Dembinsky Photo Associates/Willard Clay: 9, 29
Dembinsky Photo Associates/Terry Donnelly: 20
Dembinsky Photo Associates/Barbara Gerlach: 2
Dembinsky Photo Associates/Adam Jones: cover, 16
Dembinsky Photo Associates/Doug Locke: 19
Dembinsky Photo Associates/Skip Moody: 23
Dembinsky Photo Associates/G. Alan Nelson: 10
Dembinsky Photo Associates/Stan Osolinski: 30
Dembinsky Photo Associates/Rod Planck: 15

Printed in the United States of America.

Library of Congress Cataloging-in-Publication Data
Murray, Peter, 1952 Sept. 29-
Prairies / Peter Murray
p. cm.
Includes index
Summary: Describes where prairies are found, the plants and animals that exist there, and the role of fire in the ecosystem.
ISBN 1-56766-277-3 (library bound : hardcover)
1. Prairies—Juvenile literature.
[1. Praries.] I. Title.
QH87.7.M87 1996
574.5'2643—dc20 96-17569
CIP
AC

TABLE OF CONTENTS

WELCOME TO THE PRAIRIE!

In a city park, a soccer field, or a golf course, the grass is short and green. It is like a smooth carpet. You can run and play on it. Golf balls and baseballs roll across it easily. You can lie on your back and look up at the sky. This is the kind of grass we see every day.

When the grass starts to get long, we mow it. But what would happen if the grass kept on growing, and there was nobody to cut it? How high would it grow?

Grass on a golf course is like a smooth carpet

LONG AGO

Five hundred years ago there were no lawn mowers. There were no weed-whackers. Wild grasslands covered most of what is now the United States. From the Rocky Mountains to the Mississippi River, the land was covered with grasses and flowering plants. You could walk all day and never see a tree. In some places the grass would come up only to your knees. In other places it would be twelve feet tall!

This land was called *prairie*.

Sixty million years ago, when dinosaurs ruled the earth, most of our planet was covered with forests. Slowly, the surface of the earth changed. Continents moved. Mountains grew. The glaciers came and went. The climate changed and became drier. The great forests shrank. Where trees could no longer survive, grasses and wild-flowers thrived. Huge expanses of rolling prairie replaced the mighty forests of the dinosaurs. For millions of years, grasslands covered half of the land on Earth.

WHERE ARE THE GRASSLANDS TODAY?

Today, Earth's grasslands still cover many millions of square miles. The largest grassland in the world stretches from Europe to China Asia. It is called the *steppes*. The grasslands of Argentina are called the *pampas*. The dry, tropical grasslands of Africa are called *savannah*. In North America, we call our grasslands the prairie.

No matter what you call them, all prairies have a few things in common. The land is flat or gently rolling. There are very few trees. And there is a lot of grass!

Africa is covered with dry grasslands called Savannah

ARE THERE DIFFERENT KINDS OF PRAIRIES?

In North America, there are three kinds of prairie. Parts of Iowa, Minnesota, Missouri, and Illinois are covered with *tall-grass* prairie. The grasses and wildflowers there grow higher than your head. Farther west from Montana down to Texas grow the *short-grass* prairie. The short-grass prairie is drier and more open. It is ideal for raising cattle, horses and sheep. The land between these two areas contains a mixture of short and tall grasses. It is called the *mixed-grass* prairie.

Grasses in a tall-grass prairie can grow very high

WHAT GROWS IN THE PRAIRIE?

In one acre of North American tall-grass prairie you can find hundreds of **species** of plants, from ten-foot-tall *bluestem* grass to tiny soapweeds. Native Americans once depended on the natural prairie plants for food. Prairie turnips and hog peanuts were an important part of their diet. The flowers of the soapweed plant were used in salads. The fragrant purple bee balm flower was used for tea and perfume. More than 1,000 different prairie plants were used by Native Americans for food and medicine.

Many species of plants grow in tall-grass prairie

WHAT HAPPENS WHEN THERE IS NO RAIN?

The prairie can survive long periods without rain. The grasses have large, complicated root systems. During dry spells, the tops of the grass plants die back, but their roots remain alive. Flowering plants like coneflowers and milkweed survive by spreading their seeds. The seeds lie dormant until the rains come again.

Over thousands of years, the prairie soil grew thick and rich. It was protected by a thick layer of **sod**. The sod kept the soil from being washed away by the rain or blown away by the wind.

Coneflower seeds can survive long dry spells

FIRE IN THE PRAIRIE

During the dry season, fire can sweep across the prairie, burning everything in its path. Prairie fires are started by lightning or by people. After the fire dies down, the land looks black and lifeless. But soon the rains come again, and new green shoots appear on the blackened soil. The prairie grows back quickly. The roots of the grasses and the seeds of flowering plants are still alive beneath the surface. Fire is an important part of the prairie **ecosystem**. The ashes fertilize the soil. The new plants are healthy. Fire gives the prairie a chance to start over.

WHAT ANIMALS LIVE IN THE PRAIRIE?

The prairie is home to the biggest, the fastest, and the rarest animals. The bison, also called the buffalo, is the largest animal in North America. Tens of millions of bison once roamed the prairies in great herds. Some Native American tribes depended on the bison for food and clothing. When European settlers came to the prairies, they shot the bison by the millions. By 1900, there were only a few hundred bison left alive. Today bison are protected. Thousands of bison now roam our national parks.

Bison were hunted for their warm hide

The fastest land animal on the North American prairie is the pronghorn, also called the pronghorn antelope. The pronghorn's natural enemies are mountain lions, wolves, coyotes, and human beings. Pronghorns can run up to sixty miles per hour. That's fast enough to outrun a hungry wolf, but not as fast as a rifle bullet! Like the bison, pronghorns were once hunted until only a small number remained alive. **Conservation** efforts have helped the pronghorn survive, and today they are a common sight in the western prairie.

The pronghorn is the fastest land animal on the North American prairie

The black-footed ferret, a member of the weasel family, was once thought to be extinct in the wild. Prairie dogs were the ferrets' only food. Prairie dogs lived in burrows built in the dirt. These were called prairie dog towns. Prairie dog towns once covered thousands of square miles. Farmers and ranchers wanted to use that land to grow food and raise cattle, so they shot and poisoned the prairie dogs. The prairie dogs almost disappeared. Because the ferret needed the prairie dog for food, the ferret almost disappeared too. For many years, no one saw a black-footed ferret in the wild.

A few years ago, some wild ferrets were discovered living in a prairie dog town in South Dakota. Ferrets are still very rare, but scientists hope their numbers will increase.

Prairie dog

PRAIRIE SOIL

The prairie's most precious resource is its rich, fertile soil. When European settlers first came to the prairie, they quickly plowed the natural grasses and planted wheat, corn, and other grains. The thick sod that protected the valuable soil was torn up by plows. Natural grasses were eaten to the ground by hungry cattle and sheep. In the 1930s, there came a long dry spell. The crops died. The soil became dry and powdery. The wind picked up the soil, creating huge dust storms. Some of the best farmland in America was blown away. The southwestern prairie became known as the Dust Bowl.

Grass protects the prairie's fertile soil

WHERE HAVE THE PRAIRIES GONE?

Today, most of the great North American prairies are gone. We have dotted them with buildings, cut them into pieces with our railroads and highways, planted our crops over them, and let our cattle and sheep graze them bare. The small areas of prairie remaining are now national treasures. They are our link to the past. They remind us of the days when a bison could live its entire life without seeing a highway, a train, or a fence of barbed wire.

The prairie was once filled with bison

GLOSSARY

species (SPEE-sheez)
A group of plants or animals with similar features. Hundreds of plant species live in the prairie.

ecosystem (E-coe-sis-tem)
Animals and their environment functioning together. Prairie fires help maintain the prairie's ecosystem.

conservation (kon-sir-VA-shon)
Protecting something. Conservation of the prairie is important

sod (SAWD)
The grass covered surface of the ground. Thick sod protects the soil from being destroyed.

INDEX